Cutlass
Rules the Waves

Robin Kingsland

Young Lions

First published in Great Britain by
A & C Black (Publishers) Ltd 1994
First published in Young Lions 1995

10 9 8 7 6 5 4 3 2 1

Young Lions is an imprint of HarperCollins Children's Books
part of HarperCollins Publishers Ltd,
77/85 Fulham Palace Road, London W6 8JB

ISBN 0-00-675003-6

Printed and bound in Great Britain by HarperCollins Manufacturing, Glasgow

Chapter One

It was a slow, hot, lazy afternoon at the Cuttlethwaite Cove Home for Retired Pirates.

Marco the cook was sun-bathing,

Peter the cabin boy was listening to his pirate radio,

and Ahab the bosun was putting the finishing touches to a strange new invention . . .

It's round, and it goes up and down on this string...

I'll call it – "The round thing that goes up and down on a string".

Catchy or what??

In short, everyone on the island was in a good mood.

Well, almost everyone.

Chapter Two

No one could understand why
Cutlass Cuttlethwaite was so fed
up. You only had to look around to
see that business was booming.

Pirates who
were too old
to splice a
mainbrace;
Buccaneers
whose eers
would no longer
bucc;
Swashbucklers
whose buckles
wouldn't swash
any more;
they all flocked to
the cove for sun, sea
and a quiet
retirement.

CUTTLETHWAITE
COVE
HOME FOR
RETIRED PIRATES

SORRY
FULL UP!!

So why did the captain have a face
as long as a sea shanty? Peter, Ahab
and Marco decided to ask him.

Cutlass Cuttlethwaite stared out
across the sea. 'It's my mum,' he said.

'I didn't mean she's here,' Cutlass sighed, 'I mean I've been thinking about her!'

Cutlass Cuttlethwaite's mum, Bloodthirsty Beryl, was a fearsome, swaggering pirate. Some time ago, she and Captain Cutlass had fallen out over some treasure:

Now, give Mummy the treasure like a good boy!

No, Mum.

WHAT ??!

At the time, the captain had been glad that he had stood up for himself, but he hadn't seen his mum since that day, and recently, he had started to miss her.

I mean, she may be an underhand, underwashed sneaky cheat and robber— but she's still my mum...

And now I don't even know where she is!

Chapter Three

Meanwhile, many miles from
Cuttlethwaite Cove,
in the
Old
port
of
Bristol . . .

Mad Jack Dubloon was one hundred per cent pirate, from the patch on his eye to the tip of his peg-leg. As he slammed his tankard on the table, he complained about the terrible state of piracy.

At the other end of the inn,
Bloodthirsty Beryl sat with her first
mate, Hatchet Annie, and
complained about the
terrible state
of Mad Jack
Dubloon.

That coat
must be a hundred years
old – I've never <u>seen</u>
such a scruff !!

Hatchet Annie didn't like to hear
her boss talk like that about Mad
Jack. She liked him.

She liked him rather a lot...

She liked him so much that she
wanted to join his pirate gang. And
listening to Mad Jack going on
about being broke had given her an
idea.

Chapter Four

Late that night, as Mad Jack Dubloon was stumbling back to his ship, a hand tapped him on the shoulder.

At the end of the hand was an arm, and at the end of the arm was . . .

Hatchet Annie whispered in Mad Jack's ear.

Whiss whiss... Cutlass Cuttlethwaite... whiss whiss... Beryl's son... whiss whiss Filthy rich... whiss... kidnap... whiss whiss WACKIN' GREAT RANSOM!

'So! What do you think of my plan?' she asked.

You want me to help you to kidnap your own BOSS??!

Er....

Chapter Five

Thursday morning at Cuttlethwaite Cove was the morning the post arrived.

Peter read all his letters, then set off for a quiet day's crab fishing.

I'm off!

When he got back, he found Ahab and Marco in a state of utter panic.

This was very
bad news indeed.
Think about it.
Every pirate
who retired to
Cuttlethwaite Cove
brought a lifetime's
collected treasure
with them. It was all put away in a
locked hut for safe keeping,
and only three people had keys;

Peter, Marco and Captain Cutlass himself.

'Have you told the captain?' Peter asked.

'That's just the trouble,' said Ahab.

The captain's gone too!

Chapter Six

Peter and the others headed for the captain's hut to search for clues. They found one straight away.

Dear Crew,
I'm really sorry about taking the treasure. I can't tell you why I did it, but please believe I had to do it. I'm sorry I've let you all down. Goodbye for ever, Cutlass

News travels fast on a desert island. They were still staring at the note in disbelief when a huge crowd of retired pirates arrived outside the hut. They were in an ugly mood!

Ahab tried to calm the angry mob
by showing off his new invention.

Peter had found something. He had found:

a bottle, like the ones the mail came in,

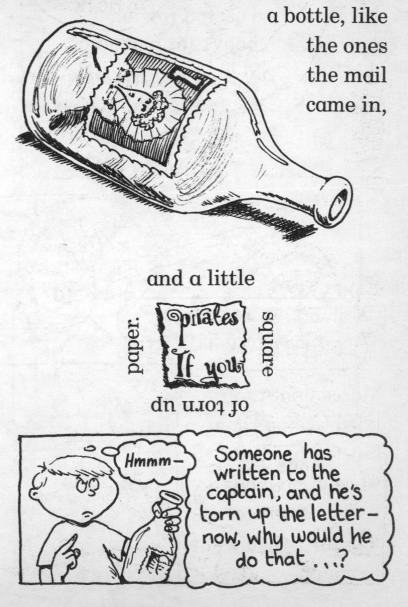

and a little

paper.

pirates
If you

square

of torn up

Hmmm—

Someone has written to the captain, and he's torn up the letter— now, why would he do that . . .?

A rumour began to rumble
through the crowd outside.
Someone had seen a rowing
boat that morning,
heading out to sea.
It could have been
Cutlass.

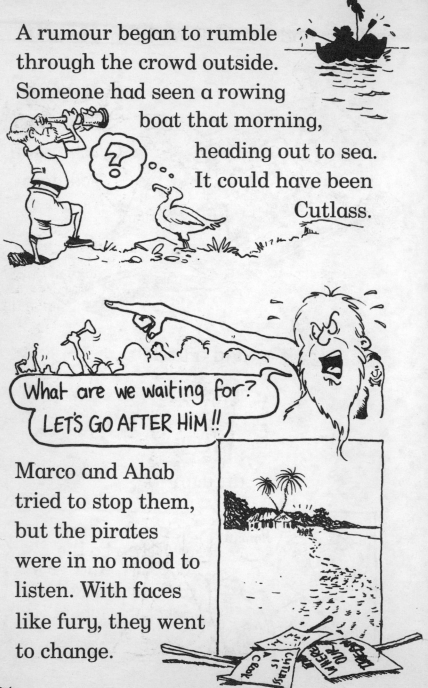

What are we waiting for?
LET'S GO AFTER HIM!!

Marco and Ahab
tried to stop them,
but the pirates
were in no mood to
listen. With faces
like fury, they went
to change.

Out went:

Just after tea that evening, three
angry galleons set off . . .

. . . to
take
revenge
on
Cutlass
Cuttlethwaite.

Chapter Seven

Peter didn't touch his supper that night. He was too worried to eat. Instead, he went to search the captain's hut one last time.

Peter stood up, and . . .

¡KRAANNG!

. . . hit his head on the parrot's cage .

29

Peter spread the pieces of paper on the desk.

Then he rearranged them, stuck them together, and read the letter to himself.

Peter ran to fetch Marco and Ahab.

Chapter Eight

The 'Black Widow' had stopped being a pirate ship when Cutlass and his friends had stopped being pirates.

Cleaning her up after all this time was a big job, but Peter, Marco and Ahab worked hard.

Rails
were
painted,

decks
were
scrubbed,

and
sails
were
patched.

Then Peter
pulled a rope. . .

. . . and the Jolly Roger went fluttering up the mast once more.

Now all they had to do was catch up
with the pirates – before the pirates
caught up with Cutlass!

Chapter Nine

Cutlass Cuttlethwaite was not enjoying himself. Bobbing about in the open sea in a leaky boat, with no more biscuits, no more water, and only a parrot for company, things couldn't get much worse.

Or so he thought . . .

Captain Cutlass hid under a sheet and held his breath. The pirate ships came closer, and closer, until:

In no time at all, Cutlass was
dragged aboard and tied up. Then . . .

Suddenly . . .

The retired pirates looked around in astonishment. They had been so busy watching Cutlass walk the plank that they hadn't even noticed the 'Black Widow' until she was right beside them. Peter didn't waste any time.

Ahem...

Before you go on, you might like to hear this...

Peter read . . .

Cassull Dubloon
Crackscullion Iyland
(Second left after Tobago, can't miss it.)

Oy! Cutliss!

Eye have took yore mum prizener!
Callect awl the tresher wot yoo
have got off them old pirates, and
bring it to my cassull. If you don't,
eye will feed yore mum to the
fishies. Eye meen it, right ?!?

Hope yoo ar well,
Lots of luv,
Mad Jack Dubloon M.P.
(Mad Pirate)

Peter looked up from the letter.
'Does anybody have anything to
say?' he asked.

Chapter Ten

It's not every day you see fifty-seven grown pirates wipe tears from their eyes, but that's what was happening. The crowd all stared down at their feet, or their wooden legs, ashamed of the bad things they had said about Cutlass. The captain was quickly untied.

But Peter knew that they couldn't go home just yet. There was another job to do first. A daring, dangerous job which would bring them face to face with

Mad Jack Dubloon

More than ever before, Peter needed a foolproof plan! Just then, he saw Marco the cook. And as soon as he saw Marco, Peter knew what to do.

Marco — what's the biggest cake you've ever baked?

Chapter Eleven

Clouds bearded the moon that night,
as a ship softly dropped anchor off
Crackscullion Island.

Gloop!

Splish

Splish

I feel sick

Shhh!

"Quietly"
he said

Moments later,
rowing boats
headed
quietly
for the
beach.

Splish!

Soon
after that,
silent figures
darted through the
alleyways, towards Castle Dubloon.

Stage one of Peter's rescue plan was
in progress.

Chapter Twelve

Bloodthirsty Beryl sat in her damp, dripping dungeon, listening to Hatchet Annie talk about her favourite subject – Mad Jack Dubloon.

He's really clever too, Beryl...

For instance, did you know he can swallow a whole **CHICKEN** in one go?

Annie had seen nothing wrong with helping Mad Jack kidnap Beryl.

Oh, I'm _so_ impressed!

Huh!

After all, her family motto was:

Besides, it had helped her to get into Mad Jack's Scurvy Crew.

The sound of the front door knocker echoed through Castle Dubloon. Hatchet Annie scuttled off to answer it, leaving Beryl to think her own dark, dungeonish thoughts.

Chapter Thirteen

Hatchet Annie heaved open the big front gate to find a cart.

'You see, it's his birthday tomorrow,' whispered the boy, 'but no one ever remembers, so his Auntie Aggie has sent this giant cake as a surprise.'

Hatchet Annie thought quickly.
Remembering
Mad Jack's
birthday would
earn her
barrel-loads of
Brownie points.
All she had to do
was tear up Auntie Aggie's card,
and write a new one – from herself!

Bring it in...

I'll make sure he gets it.

Oh, he'll get it all right!

Once the cake was hidden, Annie shooed the delivery boy out. But the moment the door slammed shut behind him, the 'delivery boy' threw off his disguise, and ran around the corner.

Chapter Fourteen

Mad Jack was getting just a teensy bit fed up with Hatchet Annie. She had been giving him funny winks and smiles all morning. And she kept running behind a big curtain in the corner to look at something. Still, he had no time to think about it now. A message had come from the main gate. Cutlass Cuttlethwaite had arrived.

Moments later, Captain Cutlass appeared, dragging an enormous treasure chest behind him.

Here's your ransom, Dubloon - now set my mum free !!

Don't be hasty, Cuttlethwaite - let's count it first!

'Oh, count it later, Mad Jack,' Hatchet Annie said suddenly, 'you must open my present first!'

PRESENT?! What's she on about now?

Mad Jack was beginning to think that Annie had cuckoos in her crows-nest. Still, he thought, a present is a present. 'Go on then,' he said, 'let's have it.'

Hatchet Annie pulled back the curtain. There was the gigantic cake. Even Mad Jack's pirates were impressed.

That was when the cake exploded.

Chapter Fifteen

SURPRISE!

shouted fifty-seven retired pirates.

Mad Jack's pirates
drew their cutlasses,
and prepared to fight to the death!

Then suddenly, everything went strangely quiet.

'Don't just stand there!' Mad Jack bellowed. 'Get them!'

Mad Jack was livid. All his blood-curdling pirates were wiping their eyes and blowing their noses and finding out how the rest of their family was.

Meanwhile, he could see Peter, Cutlass, Ahab and Marco closing in on him.

Cutlass and his friends were stuck in the crowd. 'He's getting away!' Peter yelled.

Chapter Sixteen

The talk went on until well past bed-time...

Ahab
talked
about his
invention:

I call it the "Yo Yo Ho Ho."

Hmm— It's still a bit long.

The name or the string? ARK!

Marco talked about his giant cake recipe . . .

So let's see, that's . . . a ton of flour, two tons of sugar, a hundred eggs, . . . and fifty-seven elderly pirates!

And Mad Jack talked about getting a good lawyer.

What's a lawyer?

Expensive.

But best of all,
Cutlass and Beryl
talked . . .
and talked . . .
and talked.
They hugged
and made up,

and then Beryl sighed, and declared
that piracy was a mugs game and
that she longed to give it up.

And that might have been the end
of the story . . . but it wasn't!

The Last Bit

Mad Jack Dubloon was put on trial
for piracy, kidnapping, robbery and
fishing without a licence. Everyone
thought he  was for it,
but just as the judge
was about to pass
sentence, Beryl
leapt up!

Excuse me
your Judgeness —

Would you
let him off if
he promised to
settle down?

Beryl explained further. You see,
even though Mad Jack had
kidnapped her, she could see that he
wasn't all bad – it was obvious that
Hatchet Annie had put him up to it.

Anyway, Beryl had been visiting
Mad Jack in prison, and talking
and . . . well . . .

Everyone in the courtroom cheered.
Everyone except Hatchet Annie
that is. She was furious!

But the judge reminded her of her family motto, and fined her for shouting in court.

As for Beryl and Mad Jack, they got married, moved to Cuttlethwaite Cove . . . and lived happily ever after.

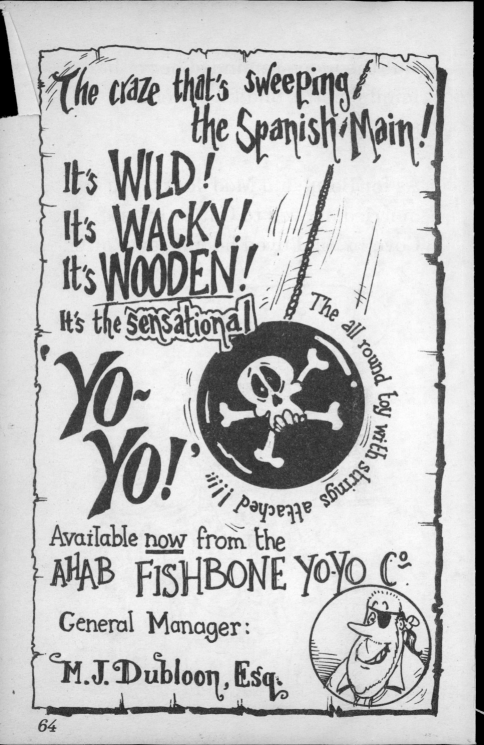